falling in Love

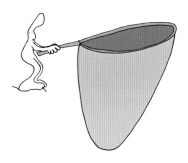

Sixth Avenue Books™ are published by:
AOL Time Warner Book Group
1271 Ave. of the Americas
New York, NY 10020

Visit our Web site at www.twbookmark.com

An AOL Time Warner Company

Printed in China
First printing: 10 9 8 7 6 5 4 3 2 1

ISBN: 1-931722-17-X

falling in Love

BY LISA SWERLING & RALPH LAZAR

Sixth Avenue Books™

An AOL Time Warner Company

Alone at his desk,
late at night,
the writer
wonders...

How do people
fall in love?

growing watermelon growing watermelon

Desperately he lowers it from
the cliff...

And it shattered
plain below...

...and dancing to t

Hmmm...
a book about Love.
How _do_ people fall in love?

Toe-to-toe, listening to the grass grow...

...and simultaneously
sneezing in the
spring of life.

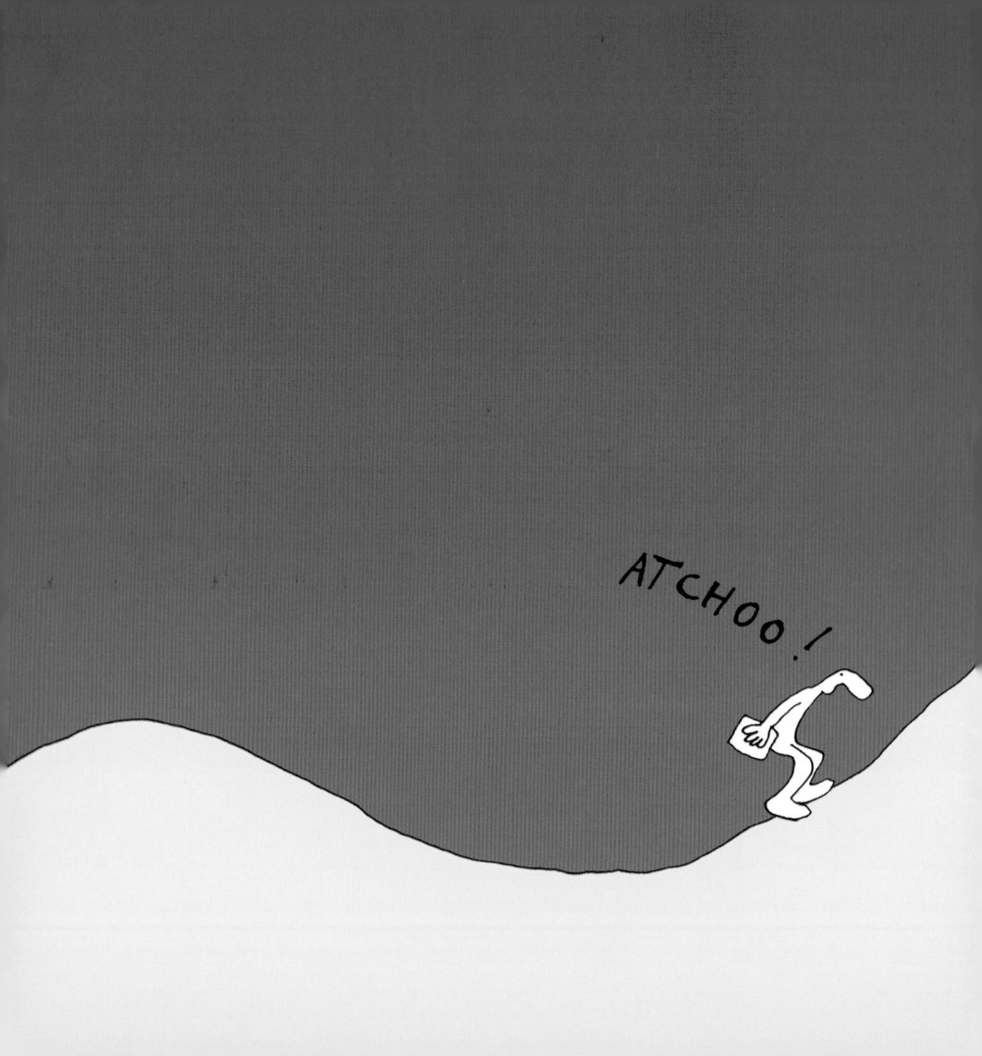
ATCHOO!

Some people
fall in love by
slipping on the
same banana
skin...

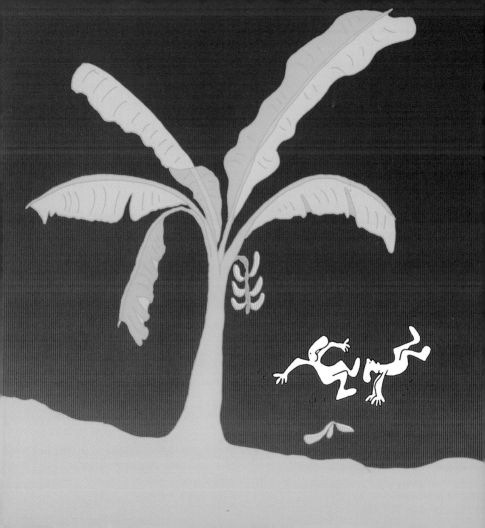

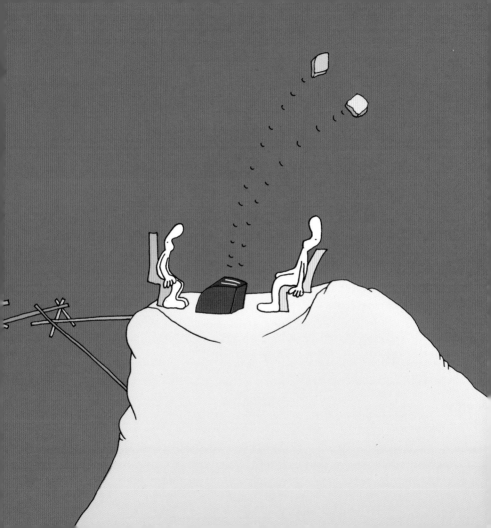

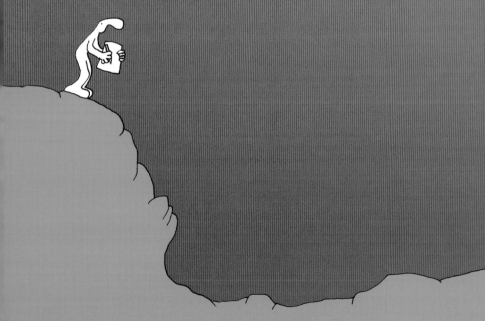

One of the things still to

be considered is the

overall effect of

the colors on

Screen as a

whole?

Hummagreeca

matte

How people fall in love:

- ☑ grass
- ☑ sneeze
- ☑ bananas
- ☑ toast
- ☑ watermelons

I think I'm getting somewhere

Hula-hooping in time...

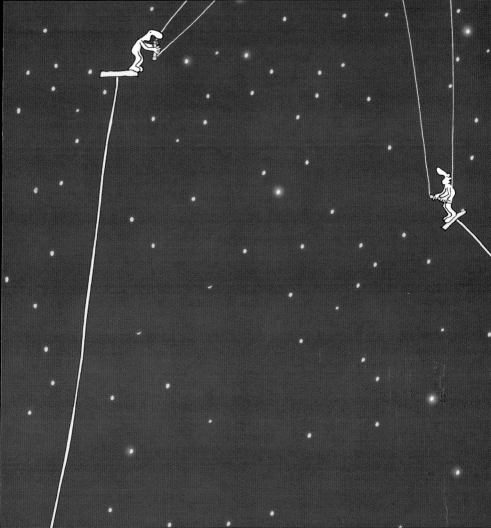

... falling
head
over
heels ...

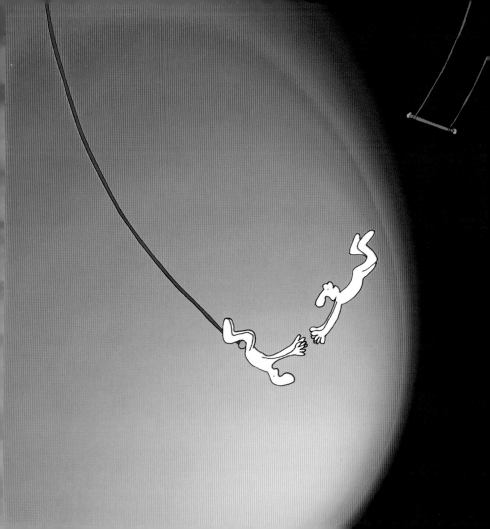

... and trusting in Fate.

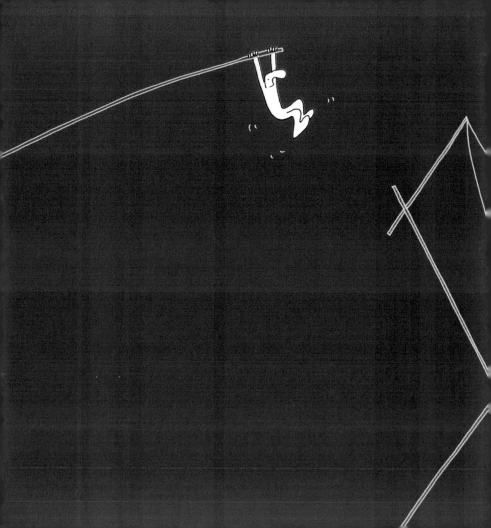

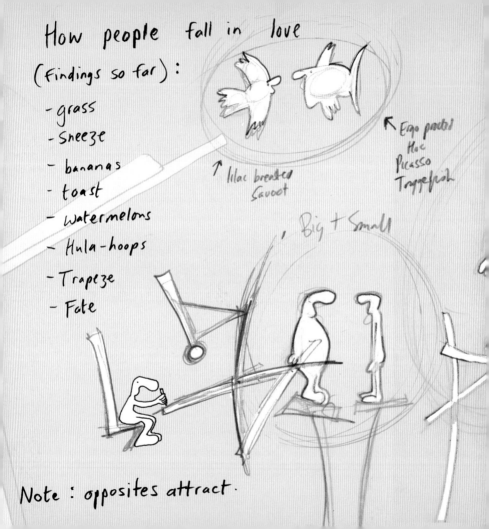

Some
just take
the
plunge ...

...ending up together
in a sea of possibilities...

...exploring the unknown...

...sharing
an outlook...

... and dreaming
the same dream.

On rainbow watch...

...painting the sky...

Gute α

Zoo Lake
Constellation

Challi Nova

Ouma + Oupa

Valli α

Morey
minor

Cleo β

Woofy
Constellation

Ga Lu...

Lignance

Caledonian Constellation

Lila

Tim ↑↓

... and talking
deep
into the
night.

Note for further research: The excavation of long-forgotten conversations

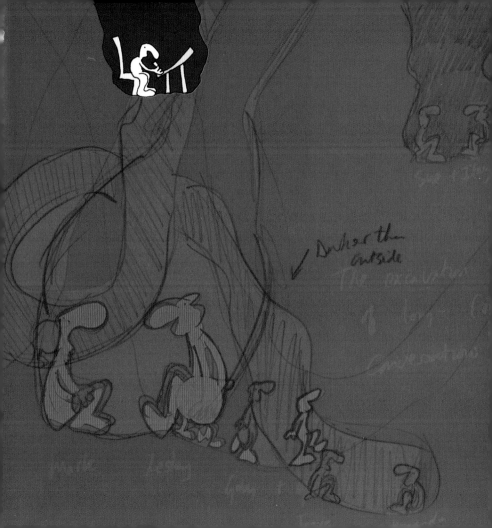

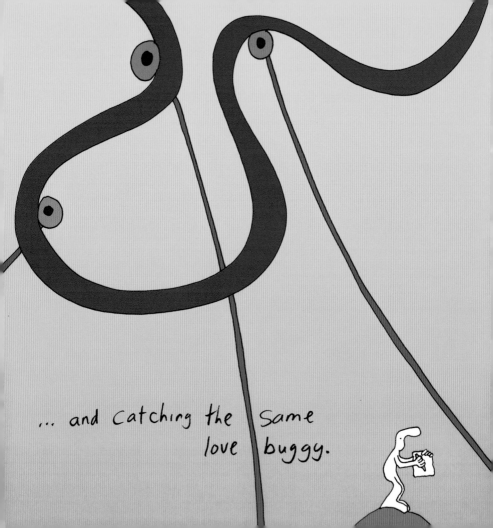

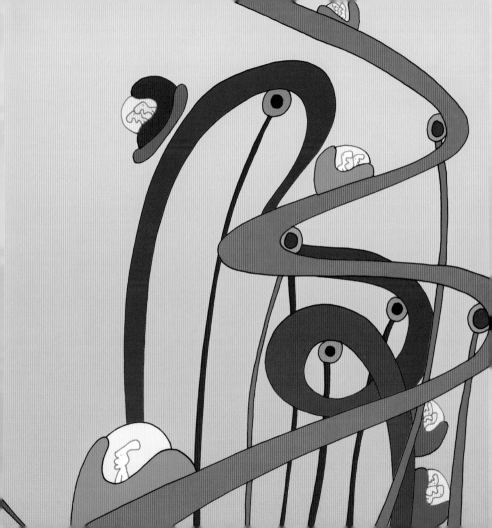

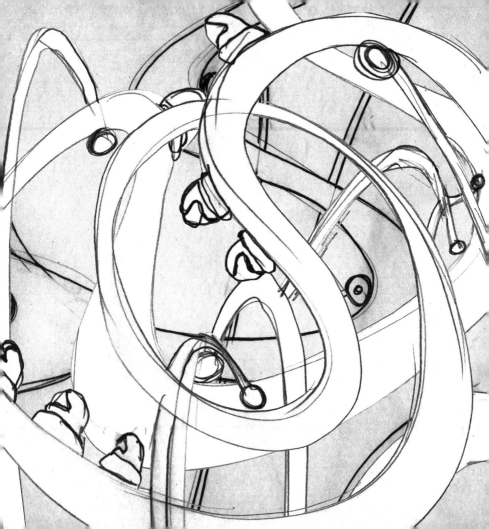

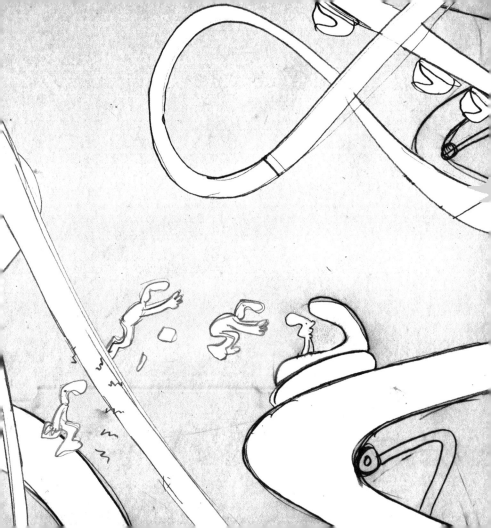

ABOUT THE AUTHORS

Ralph Lazar, Lisa Swerling and their daughter
Bea are currently based in the UK. They have
recently applied for visas to Harold's Planet,
and are expected to move there as soon as
the paperwork has been processed.

This book is for Ouma